# Jenny's Christmas GIFT

# Jenny's Christmas Gift

## JOHN PONTIUS

CFI
An Imprint of Cedar Fort, Inc.
Springville, Utah

© 2014 John and Terri Pontius
All rights reserved.

No part of this book may be reproduced in any form whatsoever, whether by graphic, visual, electronic, film, microfilm, tape recording, or any other means, without prior written permission of the publisher, except in the case of brief passages embodied in critical reviews and articles.

This is not an official publication of The Church of Jesus Christ of Latter-day Saints. The opinions and views expressed herein belong solely to the author and do not necessarily represent the opinions or views of Cedar Fort, Inc. Permission for the use of sources, graphics, and photos is also solely the responsibility of the author.

ISBN 13: 978-1-4621-1510-5

Published by CFI, an imprint of Cedar Fort, Inc.
2373 W. 700 S., Springville, UT 84663
Distributed by Cedar Fort, Inc., www.cedarfort.com

LIBRARY OF CONGRESS CATALOGING-IN-PUBLICATION DATA

Pontius, John M., author.
Jenny's Christmas gift / John Pontius.
    pages cm
Summary: A true story about a family taking a homeless teenager into their home for Christmas.
ISBN 978-1-4621-1510-5 (alk. paper)
1. Christmas stories.  I. Title.

PS3566.O616J46 2014
813'.54--dc23

2014026075

Cover design by Shawnda T. Craig
Cover design © 2014 Lyle Mortimer
Edited and typeset by Kevin Haws

Printed in the United States of America

10 9 8 7 6 5 4 3 2 1

Printed on acid-free paper

# Dedication

To Jesus Christ, the giver of
the greatest gift of all.

I was sixteen and had just gotten my driver's license. I had a little money from milking cows and selling a steer I had raised. As I recall, I had forty bucks to spend on Christmas. It seemed like a lot of money, and I shopped with a real sense of joy, looking for just the right gifts. It was the first year I got permission to decorate the tree all by myself. I proudly chose a flocked white tree with blue lights and red bows. I'm not even sure it was pretty, but it and everything about Christmas that year seemed magical to me.

On the afternoon of December 24, the phone rang. I was sitting on the couch studying the growing pile of presents, admiring my tree, and imagining what fun it would be to watch people's eyes as they opened my gifts to them. The phone rang out. My sister hurried to it and began talking in whispers. When my sister hung up, Mom motioned to Dad, and all three left the room. More whispering.

Then my sister put on her coat and drove off into the chilly afternoon.

After my sister left, Mom and Dad called everyone into the living room near the Christmas tree. They explained that my sister's friend Jenny had just been kicked out of her home. Jenny had done something to annoy her father and he had thrown her out of the house—without a coat in a snowstorm and on the day before Christmas! She had walked several miles to a gas station, borrowed a dime, and called my sister, who was at that moment on the way to fetch her. Jenny had been crying on the phone. "I'm so cold and afraid, and I don't have a place to live. Could I spend the night at your house, please?"

My parents looked at each of us with concern in their eyes. They told us they didn't want to spoil our Christmas, but they were worried about Jenny. Mom was furious that anyone would get thrown out of their home on Christmas Eve and said so many times. They told us Jenny was going to be spending a few days with us, including Christmas morning. They continued to explain that Jenny would have no Christmas at all unless we provided it for her. They gently asked if there was anything we could think of—that we had purchased for one other—that we could give to Jenny instead? We were excited to help and all started talking at once. Suddenly, none of us were thinking about our own Christmas at all.

Someone remembered he had purchased slippers and they might fit Jenny. Another sibling happily suggested giving her the coloring book and the crayons that she had previously bought. Someone else remembered a bottle of perfume. The only thing I could think of was a pair of knit mittens I had purchased for my older sister.

> Suddenly, none of us were thinking about our own Christmas at all.

We scurried about, changing labels, rewrapping, reboxing, all the while laughing and planning a surprise Christmas for Jenny. I remember being genuinely thrilled. I couldn't even recall what Jenny looked like or how old she was. She was a mystery to me, but she became the focus of everyone's Christmas joy. She was more important than anyone else because she needed us—and I realized years later that we needed her.

In those days, we didn't give big gifts. Our parents generally purchased a few lesser things and just one nice (but needed) gift for each child. These were usually practical gifts, like a coat or Levis jeans. To give up one of these nicer gifts was to give up Christmas. I recall how our parents juggled things around, asking us privately if we were willing to give our special gift to Jenny. I don't remember even considering what that would mean to me on Christmas morning. My mind was fixated upon the look of surprise Jenny might share with us when she saw there really was a Santa for her after all.

Jenny arrived at our house in the late afternoon, clutching a thin paper shopping bag to her chest that contained everything she owned. She did not have a coat and was wet and cold.

My mother whisked her upstairs, drew her a bath, and tucked her into a warm bed. I only glimpsed her from a distance for a few seconds, so Jenny remained a mystery to me.

> She was more important than anyone else because she needed us—and I realized years later that we needed her.

I had difficulty sleeping that night—just like every Christmas Eve of my childhood. In the past, the anticipation of receiving gifts had always kept me awake. That night, it was the happy anticipation of Jenny's surprise Christmas that kept my mind spinning throughout the night. Morning finally came, and as usual my brother and I got up early to milk the cows. When we returned, the family was milling around the tree, trying to read labels without actually touching the packages—because touching them was a definite Christmas no-no in our house. Once Santa put a package under the tree, touching it might make Santa take it back or, even worse, give it to a sibling. We knew that it was just a joke, and someone always "accidentally" bumped one or two packages so the tags on the bigger ones could be read. Of course, it was my parents' way of keeping us kids from exploring the tree before everyone arrived, and it *mostly* worked.

We gathered around the tree, waiting for my father to begin handing brightly wrapped gifts around. The small things would come first: candy, socks, underwear, and toothbrushes. Then after that would come the small toys, big bottles of smelly soap, puzzles, and games. Finally, the best things: pocketknives, a new dress, or something we really wanted, like a BB gun, sled, or bicycle.

"Where's Jenny?" my mother asked, looking around at the expectant faces.

Jenny hadn't gotten out of bed. My sister ran upstairs and returned, saying that Jenny was not coming down; she didn't want to spoil our Christmas. We kids stared at one other in disappointment, our hopes of watching Jenny's happiness as she opened her Christmas surprises having just been dashed. My father suggested that maybe she needed time to herself. We sat around the twinkling lights, feeling crushed. We wanted her to come down and said so.

My mother left in her "we'll see about this" kind of mother mood. After a few minutes, Jenny came down the stairs in my sister's fuzzy bathrobe. To my utter amazement, Jenny was a cute sixteen-year-old with beautiful red hair and a Grinch frown big enough to fry a camera lens. I couldn't remember ever seeing her before at Church or school. Jenny sat on a chair as far away from the family as possible, crossed her arms, and then lowered her head, her long red hair obscuring her face. My dad knelt by the tree and rummaged through the packages, finally pulling out a small gift. He read the tag. "This one says, 'To Jenny, from Santa.'"

> Jenny was a cute sixteen-year-old with beautiful red hair and a Grinch frown big enough to fry a camera lens.

Jenny looked up, her eyes becoming tearful. "It doesn't say that!" she cried. She thought he was mocking her.

Dad stood and carried the package to her. "No, it really says, 'To Jenny, from Santa.'"

She rubbed her eyes and took the small box. We all waited. She looked around the room, studying our faces for duplicity or meanness. She only saw love and anticipation. Finally, she untied the bow and opened the box. She pulled out the gloves I had purchased and carefully flattened them on her lap.

"Thank you," she whispered softly.

A couple presents later, she received another box. Before long, she was sitting in a pile of wrapping paper, her lap piled with gifts, her tear-streaked face radiant with joy. "This is the best Christmas of my whole life!" she said.

"What do you mean, Jenny?" my mother asked.

Jenny looked up. Her voice was trembling as she said, "My mother died when I was seven, and we haven't put up a Christmas tree or given gifts since then. This is the first Christmas I can actually remember."

I was stunned, as was all my family. Jenny slowly opened the last box and found a new coat that Santa had (accidentally) purchased in my older sister's size. Jenny slipped it on—and it fit perfectly.

"It's beautiful!" Jenny cried. "How did you know my size? Why did you do all this for me? You don't even know me."

My mother smiled. "No, we don't know you, Jenny, but we do love you."

Jenny wept tears of happiness interspersed with bright laughter. I don't recall what the rest of us received that year, but I have never forgotten the magic of that morning, of watching Jenny's surprise turn to joy as love wrapped itself around her soul and the beautiful, warm blanket

> "No, we don't know you, Jenny, but we do love you."

of her first Christmas with us helped thaw her aching heart. She found more than gloves and a coat in those boxes; she found a home. She didn't just share our Christmas morning; she shared our hearts.

That Christmas we discovered that the best gift of all is not given by human hands, but it can be received by the humblest of hearts: the pure love of Christ. Jenny became my sister that morning and came to live in our home. She lovingly played with the younger children, worked in the fields alongside the rest of us, and discovered her true nature as a daughter of God as she grew to embrace the restored gospel.

Jenny spent every Christmas with us until she married in the temple six years later. Our family circle was complete.

## About the Author

**JOHN PONTIUS** **is** the best-selling author of *Visions of Glory*, *Journey to the Veil*, *Following the Light of Christ into His Presence*, and *The Triumph of Zion*. "Jenny's Christmas Story" is a true account taken from his childhood in Roy, Utah, which John documented in 2010 for his twenty-two grandchildren in his popular blog, *UnBlog My Soul*. He passed away in 2012 shortly after the publication of *Visions of Glory*. Jenny's actual name has not been used in this pamphlet.

0 26575 15105 3